SEVEN NIGHTS

SEVEN NIGHTS

SIMON STRAUSS

translated by Eva & Lee Bacon

RARE BIRD

LOS ANGELES, CALIF.

Publisher's Cataloging-in-Publication Data
Names: Strauss, Simon, 1988-, author. |
Bacon, Eva, translator. | Bacon, Lee, translator.
Title: Seven nights / Simon Strauss ; translated
by Eva & Lee Bacon.
Description: First North American Trade Paperback Edition |
A Genuine Rare Bird Book | New York, NY; Los Angeles, CA:
Rare Bird Books, 2019.
Identifiers: ISBN 9781644280515
Subjects: LCSH Young men—Fiction. | Deadly sins—
Fiction. | City and town life—Fiction. | Boredom—Fiction. |
BISAC FICTION / Literary
Classification: LCC PT2721.T73715 S48 2019 |
DDC 833/.92—dc23

For M and S and for T

Dandy, you know you're moving much too fast,
And Dandy, you know you can't escape the past.
Look around you and see the people settle down,
And when you're old and grey you will remember what they said,
That two girls are too many, three's a crowd and four you're dead.
Oh Dandy, Dandy,
When you gonna give up?
Are you feeling old now?
You always will be free,
you need no sympathy,
A bachelor you will stay,
and Dandy, you're all right.

—The Kinks, "Dandy"

Through so many forms of existence, Through
"you" and "we" and "I,"
And always with persistence The age-old
question: Why?

That is a children's query. But later you under-
stand:
One bears—no matter how weary—the evil,
the odd and the eerie
By far-ordained command.

The snow, the sea, the carnation, whether once
blossomed, fell apart.
Two things have remained: The frustration
and the mark of a haunted heart.

—GOTTFRIED BENN
(Translation: Karl F. Ross)

BEFORE THE BEGINNING

I AM WRITING THIS out of fear. Out of fear of the seamless transition. Of not having noticed that I've grown up. No initiation, no final exam. I simply floated into thirty. Got all the degrees, always showed up on time, smiled a lot, not much crying, cried a little, but mainly smiled. Jumped onto many bandwagons, took a short ride, then changed direction. I've traveled to distant places.

I know my way around the world. Have spoken with a lot of people, seen a lot of images, heard a lot of voices. Stood in the wind, here and there. But what really means something to me, what I really believe, I cannot say. Where I want to go, that's much easier: up and up—the ladder is long.

I've never lacked ambition. Even in school, I was the first to class, ready for the teacher to confirm with a nod that I had scored the highest grade. When I arrived at university, I told the professors what they wanted to hear. I loved to see their faces light up when I hit the right tone at the right moment, when I referenced the theory they were waiting to hear. I betrayed my heart for them. And in the evening, washing dishes, told myself there would still be time for dissent. And I would visit Rome when the weather was nicer.

A sympathy junkie. Quick to profess things I know too little about. Dreaming of opposition, but in the crucial moment remaining silent or halfheartedly searching for common ground. When it gets loud, I cover my ears. When an angry glance cuts in my direction, I look up at the ceiling, the cracks in the paint.

And now I sit here, in the middle of the night, listening to the rain tap the windowsill. All the lights have gone out in the windows across the street. *Tatort* is over, the salmon tartare consumed. Only the occasional sight of the naked man, still caught up in his dream, opening the fridge and reaching for a bottle of milk. The white fluorescent glow hits his thighs. Otherwise, nothing but silence.

And I think, I hope, there's still something to come. Quickly, before it's too late. I have no reputation to lose yet. No art collection, no front lawn. No children who could eventually leave home, nor early fame that would later strip away courage.

But soon, very soon, I will have to decide. On a life, a job, a woman. Soon the days and meetings will pass, without changing anything. The moments will remain without consequence and the tremors will subside. There will be structure. And I will be a servant to my ambition.

I am afraid of looking back later on gray, straight paths. Of losing my emotions along the way. Of routine taking over. Of the sheltered security, of convention bringing me to my knees. I am afraid of never having raised my voice, of always remaining at a library volume, that's what I fear, sitting here at my tidy desk, with a candle and a pen, ready for dictation. The projects will come, I will be challenged and promoted. Exiled to an office with a window that can't be opened. I feel threatened to my core by the drab frame of my future life. The frame is already hanging in the upper-right corner of the white wall, ready to fit me in, to pin me into a fixed pose.

From the beginning I've had a space by the warm stove, always well fed, handed every opportunity. The opera subscription came with birth. I was born a weakling and my privileges have only made me weaker. Danger is something I have never felt. Without a clue that paths could lead anywhere but up. I am trapped in a bubble of happiness. I've fought for little. There were always enough ping pong tables between classes. When I turned eighteen, compulsory military service was abolished.

With every good grade, every agreeing nod, I've become duller: "What you're saying isn't wrong, but you could look at it in a different way." Compromises compromise. They weaken your handshake. Take the elevator too often, and you won't be able to find your way to the back stairs. You'll get stuck in comforts, lose your desire, lose the urgency.

I'm afraid of not wanting more than I have. I'm afraid I'll miss the right moment to leap. It's not enough to climb construction fences at night, pouring sand in your shoes and rubbing mud on your coat to give the impression of adventure and real risk to anyone who might visit. A torn jacket sleeve and a hickey on your neck don't make you a hero. It's not worth breaking the law just for short trips beyond the comfort zone. They don't lead into the open. They merely ensure that everything stays as it was before.

The fear of failure is nothing but a tic, a way to prepare for defeat. But the fear of compromise is the real barrier. Soon I will only lead conversations that begin with "Stress" and end with "so much to do." Will sit in lunch breaks and dream of sabbaticals and promotions.

Before falling asleep, I'll think about raises and wonder if there's enough baby food in the fridge. Clouds will drift above my head, and I'll never look up at them. Stars will fall and I'll be too tired to make a wish. I'm afraid of prenups and stuffy conference rooms. Afraid of bank holidays and the first insincere smile. Of my free existence coming to an end, of a permanent position, retirement funds, spa weekends in May. Afraid of the Curriculum Vitae, maybe.

That's what this night is about. That's why I'm writing. The only battle worth fighting is that for emotion. The only desire that counts is that for a beating heart. Too much ground has been lost to cynicism. It wraps its cold fingers around everything, blows out the last candle, locks the last emergency exit, tears down the last curtain. Cynicism is claiming victories on all fronts. And for those of us who fall behind, it's there to tend to our wounds with Nivea creme. It leads us to believe that all we need to catch up is its help. In reality, though, cynicism is hollowing us out, drilling deep into our core, extracting the precious resources that are stored there.

In its company, we are quick to laugh at others. Only later do we realize how weak it has made us. How our emotions, our sympathy, our enthusiasms have atrophied. We arrogantly believe that sheer calculation can achieve anything. In the dusty archives of reason, we too often search for answers that can only be revealed under the open sky. There is a hidden place inhabited by a secret that can be pondered, but never solved. Only purely logical thinkers can deny this. "Evidence exhausts the truth," Georges Braque said. And Claudel: "One who admires is always right."

These are the sentences I repeat to myself. A bit utopian? Perhaps. But if you live without them, aren't you missing something? You, who carry out your conversations with hands in your pockets, with shrugging shoulders while chewing gum. Treating irony as your insurance policy, your false bottom. You keep everything at arm's length. At worst, you get agitated, but never serious.

Don't you sometimes long for wilder thinking too? For ideas without structure, utopias without metrics, sharp edges and corners to get hung up on? Aren't you ashamed to not have an answer to the question: "What is an opinion of yours that the majority doesn't share?" Its goal is not provocation, but consciousness. To comprehend where one stands, and with whom.

I want to feel the desire for reality again, not just for realization. I want the courage for a bigger connection, for a whole narrative. We've admired the wrecking ball of Deconstruction long enough. Now the time has come for ambitious architects. For new developments not in danger of collapse.

Where are those of you with a passion for planning and dreaming? Why am I still sitting here alone, looking out into the dark? Enamored with the loneliness that I pretend to feel. Night thoughts on the second floor: prewar building, stuccoed ceiling, bar lock—a feeling for eternity.

Now and then, someone stumbles from the bar at the corner, yelling his drunkenness into the night. That gets the dogs from the neighbor downstairs barking. They don't know of my thoughts, the dogs. If they did, they'd keep quiet and devoutly fold their paws underneath me.

I long for community because I'm not good at being alone. Because I'm not up to the "vast inner solitude" that Rilke praised in his Christmas letter to Kappus. Not yet. The world I carry within is sustained by dialogue, by exchange, by the bat of an eye. I need conversations, glowing faces. Freedom and friendship—these words have the same root. They belong together. It's not too late to break through the virtual with a handshake, with a hug. There's still time to band together, to start a group with the name "New Sensualism." Memory can still become present.

So come to my table and fold your hands behind your head. I'm waiting for you. Because who else is still talking about sentiment? Who has a feel for their own heartbeat? Which mothers and fathers, which teachers and priests, which coaches and therapists encourage you to be overwhelmed? Who gives hope for another, wider world?

I dream of a long staircase that leads up to a secluded room. Entrance is only granted to those who make mistakes, take detours, experiment. This room contains nothing but a long table and wooden chairs. At the table is a group of would-be loners, at the fringe of the general public, only truly at home in this group. They're not friends, they're not close. Their tone is not yet trained. Their youth unites them. The criterion: Not yet thirty. And: to be a questioner, not a smartass.

To come together here means most of all: to feel friction. It is a place where gazes are returned expectantly, not deflected in tired skepticism. A place where naivete isn't looked down upon. Confident are those who have the strongest imagination, not the strongest rationality. A secret club for those who still believe in secrets.

But because I haven't found it yet, this staircase, only dream of it (but frequently!), I'm left with nothing but fear. Fear of losing what I have. Fear of not getting what I want.

It is the first gift from the gods: *Primus in orbe deos fecit timor—First the gods invented fear* (Statius). Because fear is not simply the ugly flipside of joy. It has miraculous powers, motivating people to tame their world through language, myths and science. To fit it into a clear form. To give it an expression.

Fear can lead me to suddenly get up from my desk, on a night like this, to go out onto the balcony, shy at first, with an unsteady step. The rain has intensified. The branches of the chestnut tree crackle in the wind. A few crows are perched on the roof, looking down at them with contempt: No composure, these branches, always just going whichever way the wind blows. The fear gives me courage, makes me step out to the railing, call and shout and swear with outstretched fingers: "I don't want to be a nobody."

Before the moment of transition comes, before the future can incorporate me forever, I want to break free one last time from the fixed course. I want to hang on the hands of the clock, to try to be an agitator myself. Just once I want to feel what it's like to take a deep breath, step out of the shadows and look down at the world below. I want to. And I can.

Because I have received an offer. Someone I barely know, whom I have met only recently, has sealed a pact with me. He's going to lead me, he said, where I want to go. I don't know why, but I told him everything, spoke of my despair, my deficit. And he listened, unabated, never glancing at his watch. He looked at me and led me into temptation. And in the end, after I finished pouring out my soul, he said, with a twitch tugging at his mouth, that he knew exactly what I was missing. And that he knew the way.

Every night at seven, he would get in touch to send me on a foray into the city. I would always encounter one sin, one of the seven deadly sins. "So that you may find one that suits you," he said. "Or refrain from them forever." For a night, I would have the chance to search for the storm, to cause it myself. But by daybreak, I would have to finish my writing. Until seven o'clock, seven pages, each time. I was told to think it over. I'd have a night to consider.

This night is over. Behind the crows, the sun is rising. I don't know what he wants from me, what's in it for him. This man, he's on the other side. Older than thirty. He has a life and a path. I don't know if I can trust him. But I have no excuse. No alternative. I will accept: I will be greedy and proud, gluttonous and lustful, will be wrathful, envious and slothful. I will pull seven all-nighters, to push off the moment of transition, to escape the impending future just for a little while longer.

Maybe I can only preserve my inner self by revealing it. For one night, for seven pages. The attack will make me attackable, but also protect me from too much protection. Since I don't encounter danger anywhere, I'll have to search it out myself.

I will sin. Seven times. Write seven times through the night, like I'm doing now. With this strange confidence, in this deserted silence, this spare light. No squealing tires. No ringing phone. No running washing machine. The distant is close. Almost tangible. Now I could become anything, say anything. That's how it seems. No wound so deep that I can't dig deeper. No pain so intense that it can't be the key. Only I don't yet know if what I feel at night will withstand the light of day...

But night is also a time of fear: Loneliness crawls out of the corners, chokes my soul and bites my nails. Narrows the focus back to only me, and the awareness disappears. A moment ago, I felt great, important. Now I'm smaller than small. A nothing, a nobody. Someone who pulls his nose hair and imagines his friends weeping at his funeral. Which music is played, what photograph stands in the background. At night, people don't like to be alone—not only because it's colder under the covers, but also because the ghosts don't have to pick whose heart they'll grip first.

The nighttime writer is ambiguous. Sitting on one shoulder is the fear of failure. On the other, the courage to take on everyone. Sometimes he looks across his possessions, regards the world from above, sees how to make things better, believes in the inherent thought, the deed, the meaning. Then he looks down at himself, and he's only a small piece, a cog set in motion by external forces. He sees a young man with graying temples who drops his pen.

There are opportunities that are specific to a certain age. Then you have to decide: either-or. The old game of chance. I have made my decision. I want it. Want to write the first few sentences. Want to gush unguardedly. To draw a sketch, build a model, make a wish list.

This is my first and last breath. A warmup for the short appearance before the curtain falls. These words are an instigation, but also a farewell. Written at night, to be read at night. Ideally spread out over the span of seven. They contain courage. Desire. And fear. Be careful with them. Because they could mean something.

He who sent me will remain silent for now. Only once will he speak. At the end. When everything is done.

Until then: Join me at the window. Close your eyes. And break the glass...

I
SUPERBIA

How much the world needs me. How much it depends on me. Now. Today. Here. Not tomorrow. Not later, but now.

I kick away the cups of the beggars. Pull the woolen caps from the heads of music students. Outside beer tents, I spit into the glasses of drunks. I tear the balloons from the hands of stupid kids, watch them rise into the clear night sky. Let the kids cry, let them scream and spit with anger. It only broadens my stride, swells my chest. I laugh at the fare dodgers that get busted, the man in the sausage stand caught in a cloud of smoke and the lost tourists. All the young fathers with their bikes, their child seats, their BabyBjörns, just waiting to show off how quickly they can change diapers. How very happy they are in their new role. Finally, they don't have to be a man anymore. Only a dad. I laugh at the well-behaved people on the escalators, always standing on the right, showing off how thoughtful and socially competent they are. They probably mention that in their job applications under "Community Contributions": "I always stand on the right side of the escalator (and only there)." And I laugh about all the young ones who are as old as I am. Who talk of nothing but family celebrations, keep their hands warm in their jacket pockets, but would never use their fists. Who are even afraid of tight boxer shorts and never wanted to be like Serge Gainsbourg. I laugh about them all. Long and loudly. Because I jumped, 150 meters down. Along the smooth skyscraper facade. No umbrella, no net. I didn't scream. Didn't make a noise. I kept my eyes wide open, stared firmly into the void when they pushed me over the edge. Under the bright full moon. I felt what it is like, to fall. To plunge into nothingness. Without anything to hold onto. No floor beneath me, no helping hand. What it must be like to really jump. When everything is over and despair has won out. When all group therapy, cognitive enhancement and chat rooms have failed, when the last text has been sent. As I fell, the wind slashed at my face, taking away my vision and my consciousness.

But I landed. Safe and sound. And yet, I was shaking. I threw away the certificate immediately: official acknowledgment of my victory over gravity. What a way to demystify the whole experience. I've looked death in the eye. Nothing less. His pupil was white, like a shark's just before the fatal bite. With pale and empty eyes, he stared at me and didn't blink, like a pro at that old game that children play. He briefly whispered: "Not now, but soon." With this sentence in my ear, my feet touched the ground. I put my hands on the boney shoulders of the girl who was there to catch and unlatch me. And then I ran, fast and without looking back. Off into the night. Laughing, full of mockery. Because pride comes after the fall.

At an intersection I see a few traffic cop pedestals. With their red and white paint they stand there like the last witnesses of a time in which authority was still a matter of formality. It wasn't only for the sake of visibility that traffic cops once wore white gloves and white coats. People called them "white mice." Their uniforms were more regalia of honor than functional equipment.

I step onto one of the pedestals and look around. The headlights of cars flicker through the night. When the traffic light switches to red a few vehicles gather and wait next to each other, motors running, like a panting herd. The traffic light produces a strange sensation of familiarity. For a few moments a community is formed, linked by common destiny, complete strangers falling in line. Then on command they jointly charge forward, remain shoulder to shoulder for a brief instant longer, until one breaks away and the group is forever dispersed.

My right hand touches my forehead in a salute. "One day, my son, all of this will be yours." No, wrong tone, wrong mood. Leave the father aside for today and just start with the son. Because he still foams at the mouth, like you in your dreams.

I know I could do it better. For example, I would be a better speaker than them. Not simply come up with better phrasings—many can do that—no, I could bring life to the sentences, make them sharp, so that they land and stick. Could string the words together without any space for "like" and "um". People would listen to me until the last word. I would talk like others conduct Bruckner's Ninth or commentate in a soccer stadium. Language creates reality, that is indisputable. What we need is more exclamation points again—otherwise we end up talking with no one but ourselves. The fear of set phrases and clichés keeps us silent. And the dread of the unfinished expression destroys our hearts. In our attempt to pick just the right address, an "equitable" and "easy" language, we don't notice ourselves shying away from the real thing. A few decades ago a reference to "class" could win any discourse, now a reference to "gender issues" is all you need to get everyone on your side. We're always identifying with those discriminated against. Out of solidarity, we too feel discriminated against and wait for lawmakers to step in on our behalf. But a society can't survive if no one owns up to the larger whole. It surrenders to the divisive attacks of ideologues and cynics. Our lives are ruled by apathy and retreat. We have to do something about it.

Once I gain power, I'll build public squares where people can gather and talk. Squares that inspire courage, that don't suppress. With fountains and stringed lights, last-minute accommodation and speakers' corners. Spaces that don't get appropriated by any one group, but rather remain open, agile, ready for attack. I will grow grapes and rose-mary there and install small buckets in the floor where you can cool your beer in the summer and warm your feet in the winter. And there will be enough stone benches. Nothing is worse than a square without benches. Yet, it won't just be a place for relaxation, but one that challenges you to speak your mind, take a position. It will be paradise for those that trust each other to engage face to face. Those who seek human interaction, real questions, authentic listening.

I'll dictatorially allot houses in a way that doesn't allow anyone to get comfortable in their double standards. All residents will be foreign to each other. I'll ensure that no one can make trite statements during the day, knowing full well that they'll return to the safety of their suburban villa in the evening. Forced resettlement, division of large families, fights at the tenants' assembly—bring it on if that means that everyone will get to experience foreignness firsthand.

I'll enforce that a poem must be read before every committee meeting, opening bell or editorial conference. Not a prayer, not a national anthem—a poem. Doesn't matter from which country, in which language—but it has to be poetry. That would help. For example, in preparing people's spirits for the big questions, the broad horizons. A life without coffee breaks and striking airline pilots. A poem every now and then could change a lot.

I'll appoint animals to maintain order. For demonstrations and riots, May Days and search warrants. Preferably pandas and zebras, but sometimes, when things get really heated and dangerous, giant tortoises and dromedaries. The mere presence of exotic animals would reign in even the worst offender. Their mysterious aura would intimidate him. Much more effective than any water hose. Humans are more ashamed in front of animals than their own kind. They're even shy about peeing on a tree in front of their dogs. Under my leadership there would be a close cooperation between the police and the zoo. And prison cells would get relocated to the giraffe enclosure.

I'll start academies that research emotions, not theories. Where you don't leave your heart on the cafeteria tray, where you'll feel pride in the old secret way that combines reason with emotion. Just this once, feeling would assert itself, wouldn't have to slouch off to extra tutoring, ridiculed by the rationalists, just because once again it didn't understand what the great theorists wrote about love. This would be an academy that emphasizes sensuality. Where you can drink red wine in class and write a manifesto as a final thesis. A place where you learn how to make a fire, not just how to fold the fire blanket.

On top of that—and first and foremost—I would forbid certain things. Ruthlessly and without mercy. Senior citizen travel groups, for example, who inconsiderately barge over anything in their way. Who block the most stunning views and ruin every spectacular painting with their walkers and crumpled faces. Also on the list of things to abolish: rolling suitcases being dragged down the street at 3:30 a.m., early morning chain-smokers, car alarms that go off for longer than three seconds, cryptic announcements concerning the ordering of train cars, cheerful melodies when on hold with a telecommunication service provider, cash-only restaurants, energy-saver light bulbs, adjusted opening hours, the "Classic Bell" ringtone. And much more: exorbitant prices for razor blades, printer cartridges and grapefruit juice. Oktoberfest imitations playing sing along classics, bad breath at the breakfast buffet, hair removal in the sauna and coffee stains on newspapers. There is so much to do. The world needs me, urgently. I'd just have to get into power.

The night traffic has died down. Every five minutes a car pulls up and disturbs the dark. A few sparrows have settled next to my pedestal. During my speech they plucked each other's plumage. Now they're probably having a heated discussion about my program. Most importantly, which role they'd assume in the animal security service. I hop off the pedestal and call a cab. Leave the sparrows behind and hope for a wide distribution of my ideas.

On the way home I do a stopover at the night cafe—well heated, as always. I receive messages. "Don't have time," I write back. "Very busy." Outside, life goals are rushing past. To be a pioneer, that would be something. Who would succeed at a thing like that—cutting a path into this world— if not me? A thought, a speech, a call. While still in the slipstream of youth. Before things get really serious. You'd just have to conquer your fear of sounding overdramatic.

Maxims could be thrown onto the table, banners unfurled: Risk, risk anything! And we'd start a union for aesthetic goals. Today all I did was to jump off a skyscraper on a leash. That's not enough.

I skulk home. Another day without action. Once again, only dreams of conspiracy, secret society and heroism. In Schiller's *Fiesco* there is a warning: "Our best seeds for great and good things are buried under the pressures of bourgeois life." In Bruckner's *Pains of Youth*, Desiree says: "Bourgeois existence or suicide, there are no other choices."

Out on the street I see the generations run into each other, hear their grumblings. Their hellos and goodbyes, light kisses on cheeks, as if it were nothing, as if by their mid-twenties everything was already over. And yet, this is moment to yell, "It can't go on like this!" To return the old, fiery rage (not the new, dull one) to their glazed eyes. I could be an instigator. Could stand at the podium and speak about what really matters.

Every night, on my way through the dark streets, I rehearse my speech on the abandoned pedestal. First, I let the people wait. Letting them wait is the most important thing. And then, after about half an hour, just as the mood is about to swing, I rush to the front, without a manuscript, with a half-open shirt, ready to give it all.

I have a dream. Down in the crowd I see fired-up faces. They follow me, spellbound. Cheers erupt. I turn to the side one last time, building momentum, drawing a breath. Then I face the crowd. Raise my left hand. A short murmur, then silence.

The world needs me. I'm ready. I have jumped. I have rehearsed everything.

II
GULA

New game, new chance.

The wind picks up. Plastic bags slap against advertising columns, table cloths flutter, outdoor benches creak and wobble, water slushes from manholes.

The others drive by and send hatred. From their polished folding bikes, their convertible rental cars, their colorful strollers. Hatred. Scorn. Bitterness. A man in a wheelchair, without legs, pushes the hand pedal. A blouse dress, short with green stripes, swerves out of the way and crosses the intersection. Quickly out of here.

Women in headscarves, their white faces neatly cropped, sit in an old Ford smoking cigars. Small children with helmets squeak and dally past. People pass by, their mouths covered in masks to guard against bacteria. And no one, none of them, look me in the face. Don't let their eyes stray, don't smile at me.

I've just sat down and already the waiter lays out the goods: truffle salami, beef tartare and John Stone filet carpaccio on Icelandic river stones, half-pound Pomeranian East Coast Entrecôte (Delta Dry Aged) with chanterelle mushrooms and Lecsó, third-pound Freesisch West Coast roast beef on sunchoke salad and stewed cucumber. Accompanied by a bottle of Philip Kuhn's Mano Negra, two glasses of Saint-Émilion and with the dessert of the day a clear apricot brandy. What would it be like if lust, desire and abundance ruled our lives? Instead of depression, caution and acid-reflux pills.

To casually play down the Michelin Star they got last year, the owner put up beer benches that are supposed to bring the status-conscious guests closer together. Silly idea since a beer bench is the least sensual of all seating options. Without a back to rest your arm on, without chair legs you can push back in anger during a fight. Forever trapped in the collective: as soon as one side gets up, the other falls off. Tumbles onto the ground and breaks their bones. But I am here alone, have to hold down the middle, am the sole one responsible for equilibrium.

A girl stands behind me. Skinny and dainty, large sunglasses. "Just a glass of still water please!" she calls. Her gaze is practiced, her smile deft. No carbs after 6:00 p.m. she declares, and definitely no beer or wine. Let alone Averna, the viscid remnant of German longing for Italy. Her mother is from the north of Spain, acting is something she picked up in school and now she writes novels. The first one was two years ago. Since then she's been suffering from tendonitis. And yet she tries again every morning. The taste of toothpaste in her mouth, she sits at the kitchen table and sharpens her pencils.

"Are you writing anything important?" the writer Shalimov is asked in Gorky's *Summerfolk*. I ask it, too. No, too little time, in Copenhagen she just did a performance in an old police station. She slept with and among the audience members there. Totally crazy. Free at last. A steady stream of words from a pretty mouth.

Some time ago she was dating a young singer who is now floating in space. He used to give sold-out concerts in old barns in the Uckermark. She accompanied him everywhere, helped him throw up and went with him to where kids and AA members count sheep together. But it didn't last. They separated amicably—as if that was better.

The city is big, she hadn't seen him since that very last time when they played charades in the back of a large car and dreamed of tiger blood that flowed through the cracks.

Now she gushes about Netflix and Inedia, the form of complete abstinence that Catholic nun Therese Neumann supposedly practiced for a long time at the beginning of the twentieth century. Nectar glands are said to form at the palate that supply the body. "If light is the nourishment for love, shine on!" Or something like that.

Crazy, how bright lightning is, even here in the city. When the storm clouds draw in and the first raindrops fall, people change their way of walking. All of a sudden, they move faster, more bent and sullen. The grip around the beer bottle tightens. Every German's pursuit of happiness. It's just so much harder to run off into the evening with a glass of wine, grape juice spills over and runs down your fingers like warm sunscreen.

The Blaufränkischer Zweigelt is hard to beat says Oli, the waiter with the diamond earring and an undercut. After school he did an apprenticeship as a TV technician, but then the big chains, the Media Markts and Saturns opened, the prices dropped and greed was hip. So, he changed tracks. Winery management, oenology. Oli's cowboy-blue eyes have seen the inside of every Barrique barrel in Europe and he can talk endlessly about Franz Keller. His Riesling has a creamy finish, like a Werther's Original, but with a gooseberry-like tartness. Oli's wine prose is ingenious. Only sometimes, his love of metaphors gets the better of him. Then he apologizes: "That didn't come out quite right." When Oli says "Sommelier" the first syllable sounds like he's saying "zombie." On weekends he holds tastings in discotheques. Why should only the elite get to sniff and spit? Beer pong can be played just as well with wine glasses, and of course a Chardonnay can also go with steak. "Those who measure etiquette on the color of the wine should see an eye doctor," says Oli. And also, by your mid-forties everything is over anyway.

From the other side of the street a beggar approaches my table. Proud, not demure. Wishes me a good evening with a voice soft as theatre snow and immediately breaks off as I wave my hand in a well-trained reflex. "Sorry, I don't have any change." Without even looking. The beggar punishes me with graciousness: "Have a lovely rest of your evening." My brother always says: Don't give them anything! But my sister, who is intelligent, with beautiful senses, gives freely. To every supermarket security guard and subway musician, even if they just walk down the car with an amplifier.

My heart cramps as the beggar lowers his head and turns to the next table. Contempt in his gaze, but formality in his posture. Hand resting on his lower back, ready to take a bow and patiently accepting all disregard. All the while he could just start yelling, long and loud until everyone listens, until they beckon him to their table and feed him with Dry Aged Beef and wet his chapped lips with 2009 Bordeaux.

The Freesisch beef—three weeks dry aged on the meat hook at two degrees Celsius—is the best. Oli can eloquently speak on Irish salt marshes at the Atlantic coast, on grass loaded with minerals and the special taste the meat gets from it. The same goes for the vacuum packaged lamb, which hung in the walk-in refrigerator for four months and was so tender, you could break it apart with your tongue. In his eyes, the claim that eating meat is solely a man's business is chauvinistic. Crafts and ballet are not just for women either.

A young pin-striped suit strolls past, telling his company that he's looking forward to "nesting" soon. "Nesting" with his boyfriend and his coffee machine. Tai Chi, hardwood floors and a newspaper subscription. "Nesting": Would this word have left Gramsci's mouth? Or Hemingway's? Or any other meat-eater's? No, no one who likes eating meat would say "nesting." That's a word for the contingent of folding-bike riders, long-beard cultivators and pug owners. Eating meat has become evil. Those who abstain save the world. Those who despise it eat on the right side of history. Those who salt and pepper it are viewed as incurable reactionaries. A reincarnation of Christian Thielemann with a pocket square collection in his nightstand. Those who love their filet—meaty, sinewy, marbled pieces of prime European beef—fattened up on Atlantic shores with smoked hay and warm beer—probably also favor dirty jokes and patterned underwear.

Rain falls onto the awning. No sun in sight. Pieces of Beethoven's *Eroica* drift on the gusty wind.

The other guests have long sought refuge inside, but I remain out here, eating my meat with defiant satisfaction to show the world that I am yearning. I have deliberately opened my shirt widely, let the napkin fall to the ground so that a few splashes of fat make it onto my pants.

I eat meat to become that which I'm not. Someone who does not imitate what others do. Who finds his own tone. Who has convictions and defends them against others. Who dares opening his mouth, even when in the minority. And who sometimes stays awake until the early morning, sits at his desk at the open window until the birds start singing. Someone who throws over chairs and runs into walls when he's angry. Who is seeking adventure, is brisk and honest. But because I am none of those things, least of them honest, I eat meat.

In truth I'm someone who goes doorbell ditching with a running motor. Who pushes the "Information" button at the train station and runs away. Who loves the winter and dreads the summer because that's when the sun will shine and he'll have to go outside. I'm someone who puts his socks on the kitchen table the night before to save time on the way to work the next morning. Who locks both wheels of his scooter, who takes earplugs to the concert. Who goes for a short run in the morning, only to later brag about that to himself over breakfast. That is who I am.

Someone who pretends to join the battle, but in reality would run off at the first distant cannon roll. Who praises free love only in theory and crawls back into his mother's bed at every breakup. Who whimpers when he can't sleep or misses his train. Or his writing software hasn't saved his text.

Someone who talks a lot about feeling, about better sex and fantastical alternate realities. But then just ends up watching three porn videos a day and can't even open his girlfriend's bra with his left hand. Who bolts the window at the slightest breeze and whose head sinks onto his desk at 12:30 a.m. at the latest. Who pretends to pray without ever truly believing.

Someone who throws big parties just to be at the center of things again, to be able to give speeches that he'll be congratulated on later. Who arranges poetry books on the coffee table before his friends come over for dinner. Who enjoys being generous and being admired for it. Who gains strength from the misfortune of others whom he consoles only to appear as the hero.

I am someone who even in the most caustic self-criticism remains complacent, narcissistic and self-contained. I like myself in the role of the castigated, taking myself to task without ever really questioning myself. And most importantly: without ever really changing anything. I use big words, speak of revolution, freedom, passion and quarrel. But I always keep my distance, handling the terms with caution so I can drop them if they become too heated.

I am the clandestine free rider of current events. Without a risk, without my own impetus. I let myself be taken along, I'm a part of everything, but never the first, never in charge. I arrive when all is said and done, everything is understood and everything has been decided. Again and again I lower my head and accept the facts. Like a beggar, expelled onto the street from the fancy restaurant. I will never lead an attack, a storming of the Bastille.

That is why I eat meat. To forget all of this and dream that things could be different. That there is a remaining hope for happiness, that a moment of strength, of decisiveness is possible. I eat meat to disagree with myself and my time. Every bite of raw sinew is a bite back to nature. Back to the myth, whose narrative is more enticing than that of psychology. Today, here, in this restaurant under lightning and thunder, among this gluttony, my time has come.

I eat meat. "Flesh of my flesh." When God freed mankind of solitude, he took a rib and created a counterpart. A companion from "His flesh." To find this flesh again, man will later leave his father and mother. Will turn away from his house, his youth and everything that offered him a home and protection. He will stray and search until he finds it again—his lost flesh. And then he will mature, will stand upright, will be ashamed and put a coat on his naked body. He will "cleave onto his wife: and they shall be one flesh." The old recombine anew. Reunited until further notice. The day draws closer. I have to practice—cannot fail my test. That's why I sit here and eat meat. And for this moment am a different, more courageous human being.

A man, maybe.

III
ACEDIA

TODAY I STAY HOME.

Whenever I'm alone I imagine someone watching me in my solitude. For example, when I crawl out of bed in the morning—my face still sticky from sleep—and step into the cold shower for ten seconds. I imagine this as the first scene of a movie. The opening sequence maybe. Some song playing in the background. The events on screen aren't really important yet. At least not so important that you can't simultaneously roll the opening credits in the foreground. I imagine hundreds of people in a movie theater, dry popcorn on their knees, sweaty palms shyly interwoven. They see me run through my exercise program, wheezing and lacking all discipline. Of the ten reps I usually drop at least three. Because it's either the beginning of the week or the end. Or the weekend. Because the sun is shining, it's Greta Garbo's birthday or because last night I refrained from ordering baked banana. Even though I would've loved nothing more: a soft-golden brown baked banana, still warm from the oven and dotted with honey, next to a scoop of bourbon vanilla ice cream, softly melting.

At the core of it, I despise morning calis-thenics. The whole principle of self-punishment. Senselessly straining my limbs. And for what? It doesn't make me feel more prepared for the day. That'll take its own course regardless of whether I did a few clumsy dry runs or not. And yet I do them every day, again and again, because I imag-ine them to be the start of a long story: it begins with a young man lying on the floor, breathing heavily as a small edge of sweat forms around the V-neck of his white t-shirt. He will admire it a lit-tle later in the mirror. Virile. There is a little mole on the left side of his neck. He has prominent fea-tures, nicely flowing lips. That's how it could start. And then: fresh orange juice, stock market gains, sunshine on the freshly ironed tie. A video message to the girlfriend in Tokyo, the messenger bag over the shoulder, beatboxing down the stairs, onto the bike and into the day.

That's how it could go. Could. Instead: Raindrops staccato onto the rusty window sill. No milk in the fridge, the tablecloth full of stains. On the forehead, a red pimple.

Instead of going outside, filling in the daily life like a crossword puzzle, today I'll stay at home. In this apartment that no one enters with any special expectations anymore. The apartment that is filled to the brim with habitualness.

It's also been a long time since I've been in any other apartments. What a great feeling to climb the creaking stairs with a girl for the first time. Not knowing her name, just following her footsteps. I've always enjoyed that the most. More than everything that comes after—this moment in which you know nothing about each other, could imagine anything. How the dish towel is hung, if there are matches or a lighter on the kitchen table, what is next to the bed, how many shoes are in the hallway, which pictures above the sofa, which brand of toilet paper on the shelf…

When I come to a new apartment after a successful night out, there's always a moment when

I step up to the window. Doesn't matter if it's 3:30 a.m. and my head is swimming, if I ruined some kind of mood or missed my chance. I step to the window and look out onto the street or into the courtyard. Sometimes I even light a cigarette. Just in case someone happens to look up to the window.

But now alone with my four walls. Without any milk. From the outside, voices waft in. The evening is gray as are so many. Of course everyone is dreaming of parties. But I, sitting here on my old Italian sofa with my back to the windows, am trying to find a position in which I can sit for longer than four minutes. A position in which my foot or arm doesn't keep falling asleep, in which my leg doesn't tickle and my nose doesn't run. I'm fervently waiting for laziness to arrive, to wrap me in her thick blankets, as I'm perched here, staring into the empty room that lies pale in front of me—and I see dancing couples. I see laughing faces and hear wine glasses clinking, and I see all the exuberant life that would fit in here.

I am afraid of empty rooms. Am not good at tolerating silence. I am constantly afraid that the quiet mass of unread books on the shelves will suddenly erupt in resounding laughter. Could convict me as an impostor, as a connoisseur of back covers.

The phone rings. Finally. A survey concerning new electric cars, just five minutes, please, a lot depends on it. The future of the environment, for example. And the future of the automotive industry. And last but not least, the caller's contract getting extended, he adds imploringly. So I let him ask. And why not. The first voice of the day and it already demands so many answers. If I drive fewer than 100 kilometers per day. If I would pay more than 40,000 euros for a car. The location of the nearest charging station. What I do for a living and how many people are in my household. And finally, whether I 1) live in a rural area and work in an urban one, 2) live in an urban area and work in a rural one, 3) live and work rurally or 4) live and work in an urban area. Or both or something. Short pause. I ask him to repeat the options. I still don't find an answer. Panicked, I hang up. To calm down I walk into the closet. When it comes to my living situation, I think I mostly live incorrectly. That would have been the right answer. But that wasn't an option.

I'm not home alone very often. Most evenings I have visitors, and during the day I tend to avoid my apartment. At night I lie in bed behind locked doors. Otherwise I'm out a lot, filling my days with appointments that make me seem busy and suppress the wanderlust. And the fear of an early death.

Even the feeling of sitting here during the day, when everyone else is gone and at work, makes me nervous. In the past, the house was the epitome of the workplace—at its root, the word "economy" means household management. Business was conducted not in the city but at home. At home, money was earned and important decisions were made. Outside, in the squares, there was only talk and quarrel. Under these circumstances I would have liked to stay at home.

But today on the sofa, time runs through my fingers. My thoughts are stuck in loops. I hear barking dogs and shouting owners. Car radios, screeching tires, fire trucks. I lie on the sofa, wishing it was the beach. "The most cruel thing about dreams is that everybody has them," Pessoa once wrote. I can't get this sentence out of my head.

I switch from the sofa to the armchair. Turn on the cranky old TV. It's bitter about its status as a has-been. In the old days, people gathered around it. Regarded it as a window to the wonders of the world. The entire living room was designed around it. Tables and chairs were relocated. Shelves pulled off the wall. Carpets installed. Today, everyone carries the wonders around in their pocket. They watch the most gripping movies, the most important finals on teeny-tiny screens. I buck the trend. Push the dusty button and once more blow into the embers of the dying campfire. Somewhere someone important is giving a speech concerning the state of the nation. He addresses me with a clear voice, as if I, here on this armchair next to the foggy window, am his only listener. He is talking with a lot of energy and doesn't use air quotes around his sentences:

Foreigners are dangerous. A danger to everyone who thinks that their life could go on endlessly like it has up to this point. Those who cannot imagine that things can fundamentally change. Who still hope that what's in the paper has nothing to do with their cereal bowls and tennis classes.

The foreigners are our business. They will challenge us, limit us, scare us and change our minds. Many of them are sick from what they went through, got infected with the dangerous virus of memory. They, who now live among us, in our communities and cities, who shower here, eat here and cry here. They, who make mistakes and are angry, have a true fate, not simply the wrong life. They are jetsam. If we each confine ourselves to our homes, draw the curtains, keeping to ourselves, without a counterpart, things will not work out.

For a short moment the light bulb above my head flickers. As if trying to pipe up angrily. It wants to chime in that the home in and of itself is not to blame. A person without four walls is a person without hope. Those who don't want to stay at home, who don't occasionally crave solitude and quiet, are out of their mind. Says the lightbulb to the guy on TV. Says the lightbulb to me. And the guy keeps talking at me, and at the lightbulb.

A community only stands together if its members feel responsibility for each other. In ancient Rome, patronage was not just a means for the powerful to win elections. It also secured the existence of the poor and helpless. They subject themselves to the protection of their patrons and trust that they'll be defended by them. Even in the oldest sources of Roman law, this alliance of the unequal is sealed with an oath: Patronus, si clienti fraudem fecerit, sacer esto. If a patron deceives their client they will be forever denounced. Banished. The mechanism of Patronage, which in our ears sounds like exploitation and humiliation, integrates newcomers and foreigners into a community. The relationship between the patron and the client is reciprocal: it includes freedom, security, rights and duties.

How did the speaker land on ancient Rome? What brings these big ideas to my small apartment? And how do they concern me? All I'm doing is lying around staring at the wall. And I'm hungry. In the fridge there's an open yoghurt and half a bottle of eggnog. The tube of tomato paste has sat open for too long. In the cupboard there's a bag of salted pretzels. They're no longer crunchy, but at least the salt is still salty.

One could also say that community breeds dishonesty. If there are more than two people in a room, at least one of them is lying. Or at a minimum, not speaking as freely. Keeping quiet in the decisive moment, playing down their insecurity with a joke, trying to talk themselves out of responsibility, rather than into it. Groups are dangerous, I think, then shuffle back to my armchair. Meanwhile, the man on TV has been talking in the background all this time. As if he didn't care whether someone was listening to him or not.

What we need is a modern system of Patronage. The Roman empire was only able to grow as fast as it did because it understood how to tie in its new citizens and control them through these ties. The territory was not managed through surveillance and punishment, but through the feeling of mutual dependency. We, too, must relearn the value of the personal relationship. It would be sufficient if every foreigner coming into our country was allocated an established resident patron. The state itself is hard to befriend. Its character is too stony. The constitution and the famed values cannot be touched, cannot be hugged. But the relationship, the promise between two people, creates trust across the borders of culture and morals.

I, for one, trust nobody. I don't even know my neighbors. When I moved in they didn't introduce themselves to me. And I don't knock on other people's doors out of principle. You can see that people want to be left alone. To their own devices and their delivery people. The secret motto of us all: "I would prefer not to." The pretzels are gone. On the windowsill a bottle of red wine. A gift from happier days. From a woman I don't know. On her shoulder she had a tattoo of a fern. She was accompanied by a friend from school, talked little, knew a lot. Where does she live now? Whom does she love now? City or countryside, dog or cat? Sickness, kids, frozen eggs?

Strange how the thoughts come and go. How they emerge from dust bunnies, briefly take shape and then turn into shadows again and disappear. The talkers on TV of course have to pretend that they are the masters of their thoughts. But that's not true. In reality our thoughts are the ones ruling us. Completely.

To be a patron or a client would be a duty, not a choice. One side would be incentivized with an improved chance of acceptance and material support. The other with an alleviation from certain obligations. Such as the solidarity tax or the motor vehicle tax. A lot would be gained from citizens being given the choice: pay or form bonds and once again find a reason to organize community themselves.

The bulb flickers again, illuminating the dandruff on my pullover. Cashmere always shrinks in the wash, which is why I just let it air out in the wind on the balcony. If I use the wrong shampoo, my head sheds like a blackthorn bush. Gently I brush the dandruff off my shoulders. First the left, then the right. But just moving my head causes new flakes to fall. I should wear pullovers in lighter colors. Should always make sure to stock up on the right shampoo. Dandruff is a sign of decay and neglect. I know that. But then I think, here at home nobody can see me anyway. Here at home the flakes are just stars on a dark blue backdrop. And most of all, they are mine, so I can't be angry at them.

The bulb twitches and burns out. Power outage. The TV screen goes black. On the walls I see unfamiliar shadows. Patterns form like a cryptograph, coming from the apartment across the street, where a young woman in an apron keeps passing from the kitchen to the dining room, repeatedly obstructing and revealing the light from the floor lamp. She's probably serving the main course of a dinner party. The guests are still all chipper and she's in the best mood. But not for long. In a few hours everyone will be gone and all that will remain will be the dirty oyster cutlery. Then she will be lonely as well, left with the sadness known by everyone whom time has wounded.

Once I had dinner with my nemesis. He repeatedly humiliated me, even slept with my girlfriend. He hated me. I hated him. "The enemy is our own question personified," someone once wrote in my yearbook. So I invited my nemesis. On a winter night he came running up the stairs, wheezing, sweating from his ears, not taking off his snowy shoes. We were sitting on this very sofa, the one I had just been lying on. His big butt exactly where my head was just resting. The things furniture has to put up with sometimes! I hope its memory isn't too good.

I made lamb for my nemesis and opened a bottle of Barolo. He spent the entire evening talking about the intrigues of work colleagues. I kept refilling his glass, imagining him talking about me the same way behind my back. Couldn't get rid of the image of him unzipping his pants as my girlfriend sat on the bed in front of him, hands on his hips, eyes glowing.

After the second bottle, things improved. After the third we were wasted. By the end we were sitting on the floor, shirts open, reading Celan's poems to each other. "Breath-crystal, what a word!" the nemesis said. This is how we got closer.

A day on the sofa in front of the ticking clock. Nothing attempted, nothing achieved. Just waiting.

Lange Ziit the Swiss say, by which they mean both boredom and longing. "I have *lange ziit* for you" means "I long for you." Only those who are bored can experience real longing. A life that never postpones will always be panting, never breathing freely.

Of course, you can therapy away all slowness, all that quietly cheerful laziness. You can become a workaholic and celebrate your birthday in the office. But that dream of freedom and fear of missed opportunities will remain. "I was eleven, then I was sixteen. Though no honors came my way, those were the lovely years," Truman Capote once reminisced.

When I'm alone I always imagine someone watching me being alone. I act out my life for an unknown viewer. Who sits there and notices every move I make. He knows me well by now, knows my weaknesses and strengths. I do my morning sit-ups for him alone, as well as the rhythmic movements of my hands when listening to music. I would love to meet him someday, my observer. Maybe he could offer a few tips on what I could be doing better. So far, he hasn't come forward. But I'm sure he'll call. Until then I'm going to hang out at home a bit. Look at the dancing couples and the silent shadows. And wait.

IV
AVARITIA

THE TROUBLE IS NOT losing. The trouble is that others win. The clueless beginners, who check the first box that appears in front of their chewed pencil. Who are here for the first time and immediately think they've figured it out. "Exacta two and four" they call out to the lady in the betting stand, even before the first race has started.

One of them is next to the stairs that lead up to the grandstand. He belongs to the tribe of harmless barbarians of the twenty first century. He is a super daddy. The baby on his arm, the shoulders relaxed, the shoelaces of his Timberlands untied.

Dress code: guileless wealth. I'm a little bit offended that they let someone like him place a bet here. That someone like that in all seriousness can say: "Ten Euros on *King's Soldier* coming in first."

Instead of pointing out the dangers of gambling addiction post facto ("Ask us about the leaflet, *What to do when everything is gone. Ways to escape gambling addiction.*"), there should be more warnings targeting betting newbies. A horse race bet is no family picnic. It's for risk takers, for people who order extra-spicy on the menu—not for those who gorge on their kids' cotton candy.

Prince of the Nibelungen, the horse I bet on, didn't win. Well, it didn't just *not win*, it came in last by a long measure. I had placed such high hopes in the three-year-old stallion from the Puetz stable. With a father named *Tertullian* and a mother called *Nightbitch*, how could you not? Such a risky mix of intellect and lewdness is bound for greatness. Except, it wasn't. Ninth place for *Prince of the Nibelungen*. First place for *King's Soldier*. Super daddy screamed in ecstasy.

In between the races, in the stables, jockeys sucked on orange slices. Wispy lads with milk-white skin who carry the fate of so many in their hands for a short time. For a few minutes, all eyes are on them. They become close allies.

In their fluttering wind jackets, white pants and protective goggles, they look like forgotten extras from an old movie. On the way from the show ring to the judges' tower they flirt with the stable girls who are having trouble holding the nervous horses by the halter and leading them to the race track. They're pulled back and forth by the horses' abrupt movement, knocked into the hedges on either side, whipped by their tails. Annoyed, they try to keep their own ponytails in check. Since for them, too, it's about keeping composure, giving an impression of superiority, just like the jockeys, who calmly kneel on top of the fitful animals, clean their racing goggles and keep bending down to whisper into the girls' ears: "Your bra has come unlatched, Marie," I hear one of them say. Another quietly asks about the next massage. As soon as they've passed the club stands, the girls unhook their lunge lines and jump to the side. The jockeys stand up in the tight stirrups, lean forward like ski jumpers just before the release and gallop away. Their skill is to disturb the horse's stride as little as possible, and yet in the decisive moment, slacken or tighten the reins a tiny bit. This demands maximum concentration. Their butts pointed toward the sky, almost titillatingly so, as if they were waiting for a desperate wind god to give them a slap. Potentially that's exactly what decides victory or loss in the end.

In the second race I bet an exacta on *Seagörl* and *Wild Approach*. The British jockey of *Seagörl* just won with a lower-rung horse. *Seagörl* is a descendant of the famous *Sea*-family, I read in the betting magazine that I borrowed from an old man with a stiff leg. She has a first class heritage, a purebred. Besides, she's coming from the Görlsdorf stable in Brandenburg. I seem to remember having read at some point that the stable belongs to Scientology, but I can't remember exactly. I bet only two euros, the twenty earlier were gone far too quickly. Now super daddy has my money and is investing it in Nutella crepes for his family.

The only way to gain access to the grandstand is having a VIP ticket. But if you're mumbling something about "business" and "important call," the tan security lady will let you through anyway. She knows what you're up to, but occasionally wants to take a break from being a downer. Especially because the seats in the panorama lounge are never fully occupied anyway. This is where the insiders gather, those who don't want anything to do with the agitated novices down on the picnic grounds. Here you'll come across old ladies with cream-softened hands, single gentlemen with sharply-creased pants. Arms loosely crossed, eyes directed downward even after the starting signal. This isn't the real beginning. It's too early to invest in movement. Only when the horses enter the final curve, when there are four hundred meters left to the finish line and the mob down below has started screaming and clapping, when the ground softly vibrates. Only then will they lift their gaze, scoot a little forward on their cushions and reach for their binoculars.

This is when the decision is made and we find out who managed their horse's energy well, who can still count on a final push. Now the jockeys have lost their stiff posture. Their butts sway back and forth, their panting is muffled, crops slapping fiercely. One horse stumbles, sends his rider diving into the floodlit grass. He rests for a moment, groggy, wishing he'd stayed in the rusty deck chair by the lily pond in his father's garden. Then he laboriously gets up and hobbles to the side. Over and out. Only an instant ago, hundreds knew his name, would have offered him anything for a victory. Now he is already forgotten.

The others gallop on as the crowd roars. That's roughly how it must have been in the Roman arena as the gladiators begged for a raised thumb. A "like" that decides between life and death.

Two hundred meters until the finish line. "Just based on her breeding she has a good chance," a man beside me murmurs. The key to his Mercedes hangs on his belt loop. Who is he talking about? "Who are you talking about?" Indignant "shhhhs" from the background. *Seagörl* is in fourth place. *Wild Approach* even farther down the list. No luck today. Further down I see somebody raise their fist. Super daddy.

Such behavior can't be rewarded. I've seen him copy from his neighbor at the betting stand. Shameless. I mean, there are a lot of factors to influence someone's bet: general odds, for example, reflecting the majority opinion about favorites. They flicker across the screens fifteen minutes before the race starts and many of the betting folks follow them slavishly.

I don't care much for the majority opinion. It drives me nuts when too many people think the same thing. When there's talk of a "we," I feel provoked. I prefer sitting in my own boat, am willing to sink in it if necessary, just to avoid tasting the same words in my mouth that a million others have spoken.

"When everybody is in agreement, we start doubting." I saw this silly tagline on a banner hanging outside the headquarters of *Der Spiegel* during a harbor cruise in Hamburg. I haven't been able to get it out of my head since. That's why I often say things, even if I'm not completely convinced of them myself, as long as they surprise the person I'm talking to.

The well-adjusted, the opportunists, the softies and Dalai Lama imitators: They look to the odds when placing their bets. On the other side are those forever loyal to the emperor, those who could never work up the enthusiasm for the utopian core at the heart of democracy. Who think it is enough if a few keep the shop running and make sure that the price of bread doesn't increase. Those are the types of betters who sit in the lounge with their sports magazines, who placed their bets first thing in the morning. They've aligned themselves with the various experts, offset them against each other, done the math and created clever combination bets. Simpler minds often make their decisions based on the looks of the jockey or the eye color of the horse. Academics and the nobility often are influenced in their selection by the horse's owner having a doctorate degree or a nobility title. Conspiracy theorists claim to see a connection between the nail polish shade on the lady in the betting office and the colors on the winning jockey's jersey. At every race, they say, one of the betting office employees wears the winning colors.

As absurd as these criteria are, simply copying the neighbors ticket is by far the most objectionable. It's cynical and dishonorable. But what does that mean to the modern super daddy?

Anyway, *Seagörl* is behind. A hundred and fifty meters to the finish line. Time is running out. Above the old red brick building the German flag flutters in the wind and asks itself why. Why let yourself be pulled up every day if no one looks up to you?

Something is happening. *Seagörl* is at the front of the pursuing group. Peels away, storms to the front, mud splattering. A hundred meters to the finish line. A hundred meters.

Downstairs, the stable girls are screaming, picnic blankets are flying. This would be the most opportune moment for pickpocketing. A girl with Down syndrome excitedly hugs her caretaker. Come on, *Seagörl*! For a few seconds the animal becomes my private property, all standards of ownership have faded. If at this moment Satan were to suggest a Faustian pact—my soul, a lifelong government bureaucracy job, for *Seagörl*'s victory—I would not hesitate. Avarice has taken hold of me. I want to win. Whatever it costs.

The last meters to the finish line. *Seagörl* is even with the leading horse. The jockey whips the crop against her back. Again and again. And then, it seems to work. *Seagörl* takes a leap, extends her forehooves, the first across the finish line. For a moment calmness takes over. I feel a great lightness, like sometimes happens during guided meditation. *The thoughts pass like clouds in the sky. In the distance you can hear the waves rolling, back and forth, back and forth.* Even before checking the results my gaze falls on super daddy. Previously, his arm was raised in victory. Now it hangs limp by his side. What a divine picture. A foreshadow of doomsday. Triumph, trumpets, tricolor!

Then, from the corner of my eye, I see the second place being displayed: *Wild Approach*. I shudder and stumble off the grandstand in a daze. Down on the track guys in red vests are smoothing out the ground. Soon, nothing will commemorate this momentous final spurt. At the betting booth I cash in. I bet two euros and get forty-two. The rush of victory only lasts a short time. Too short. Then I realize what I missed out on.

What if... How much would I have won, how many people would I have called up ecstatically if, instead of the two euros, I had bet two hundred?

Or at least twenty? There is no one to blame for my stinginess but super daddy and his impertinent post-heroism. If I hadn't seen my twenty euro bill defenselessly tucked into his sweaty goody-goody hand at the crepe stand, I would have shown more courage.

It's starting to drizzle. The horses in the stables are getting agitated. The old wooden displays from the nineteenth century rattle in the wind. I wonder if the British investor who now owns this race track sometimes places a bet, too, to pay for the repair of the old brick buildings? Maybe he is the well-dressed man there in the back. The one with the delicate, rosy features. He didn't get up from his bench during the race. With his back turned to the screen he's waiting for a better future to tap him on the shoulder. There is something provincial about nobody betting the big money here, all these small minds, thinking they'll walk away with serious cash after having bet fifty cents.

Later that night I bet on the victory of *Loulou's Jackpot*, putting my trust in the jockey with the white hat. For second place, I hope for number ten: *Nemesis*. Nemésis is how the commentator announces it. If your name is constantly mispronounced and you can't defend yourself—

that would have to adrenalize you, to spur you on to show them all. I hope.

Nemesis remains in the back of the middle and a pimply fop in an old top hat turns to me shortly after the finish: "Kindly give me a light."

All around me, people are already thinking about the next race, but my thoughts remain with my missed chance. This one race, this one horse. *Seagörl.* My girl. That's what could have been.

The speakers blast the Spanish national anthem. The longest race of the night just finished. 3,200 meters for horses aged four and older. The favorite, a premier long distance horse from the stable of a Saudi prince, didn't win. Justice, at least for once. Those who don't let their women drive at home shouldn't let horses run abroad. Such a double standard in terms of horsepower is unacceptable. The chatter about bribes from the sheik and corrupt veterinarians doesn't last long given the disappointing fifth place of *Elvis*. The aerodynamic blinkers don't seem to have done their job.

Shortly before the last race, one of the horses breaks free and runs across the track. A gaggle of stable girls fans out to catch it. Their efforts of calling its name and swinging the lunge line remain futile. In the meantime, I place a bet (last attempt, all in!) on an underdog that gets disqualified before the race even starts. Tristesse royale.

I say goodbye to my loyal ticket stand lady and shudder at the thought that she knows the extent of my defeat. "Thank you very much," she said amicably every time I handed her a ticket. And probably she thought: "So stupid." Then I visit super daddy for a last time. Bills are settled at the end. After each feast comes the cleanup.

There he sits, the happy camper. Of course he's not sitting on the bench, but on the backrest, his feet on the seat, the toddler on this bouncing knees. "Feet off the seat," I want to say, but then I remember that the guy is at least fifteen years my senior. For garden gnomes like super daddy, worse punishment is in order. For example, disregard. At some point this will hurt him more than any rude word I might now address to him. At some point he will writhe in despair over the memory of me silently walking past him at the end of this long evening at the races.

On his way home he will raise his pink handkerchief triumphantly into the wind. Next to him, his Swabian girlfriend and the sleeping child in designer clothing. Happily ensconced in their electric car as I miss the train and have to take a cab to the ATM. That's how it will be. Today.

But soon, I'll become somebody, and he'll tell everyone about that night in March when I just walked past him. And he will write to me and beg for a single small word for him, so that he can brag about it to his anorexic children. I will win on all accounts. I will triumph. Not today, not tomorrow. But at some point. I will save my smiling until that day. And continue betting. Every Sunday, come rain or shine…

And when death shows up at my dining room table, unannounced, without notifying my guardian angels, I will say to him: I know the horse to bet on. It's standing in the back of the paddock. It only lifts its head for those loyal to the king. Stefan George's verses are written on the hooves: "Past glory bears gifts, albeit late / The spirits inevitably return with full sails / Back to the land of dreams and of legend."

V
INVIDIA

MOST LIKELY, WE'RE NOT sufficiently possessed by the devil. Most likely, we're missing what once was the mantra of youth: rage. That and proper stationary. How much was being read— and loved—in the old days. These days we're constantly running out of time. A visit to an art show has to be prepared weeks in advance with save-the-date emails. Again and again, I tried to read Musil's *The Man without Qualities* with three others. We never made it past the first pages. And the Walter Benjamin reading group I stopped after three and a half meetings. There was always something else going on. These things must have been easier back then, in turtlenecks, smoking cigarettes. Or when Theodor Mommsen climbed the library ladder at night, candle in hand. Allegedly his white hair was the first to catch fire, then his forty thousand books. Among them a manuscript that was over a thousand years old. The famous historian had it recklessly sent to his home. The fire consumed everything. Maybe even the fourth volume of his *A history of Rome*. Or maybe he never wrote it? Even Nietzsche, who despised the Prussian intellectual, was shocked: "Have you read about the fire at Mommsen's? That all his excerpts are destroyed, potentially the most important preliminary studies made by any living scholar? He is said to have plunged into the flames again and again, until they had to overpower him—already covered in burns—with force." The next day Mommsen's students searched the rubble for remnants, collected charred papers and glued them together. They didn't want to just give up on the last artifacts of universal scholarship.

What kind of a time was that, when the papers were still white and the screens black, when it still meant something to step outside onto the street, into the bars and apartments of strangers?

Departure, resistance, slammed doors—I bet nobody asked for sparkling water back then.

What we're missing most of all today are real spaces. We let ourselves be evicted and fenced into places that were once useful precisely because of their absence of purpose and order. The library where I'm sitting right now, for example, is nothing but a service station.

Instead of bookshelves, I'm greeted by information desks and screens. Everywhere I have the opportunity to extend my membership, get information about dental hygiene or return Club Mate bottles. There's a repair cafe that revives defective electronics. Sewing machines stand at the ready to mend torn pants, and on the third floor there is a 3-D printer and a recording studio. The Ministry of Health advertises a workshop and there is a poster for a drone flight show.

Downstairs, in the family area, where kids jump around on digital playgrounds and play computer games, there's a gong that sounds when a new baby is born in the maternity ward of the city's hospital.

But the books, those stand on the sidelines. They don't fit into the image of the modern architecture of emptiness. That's why they're being relocated and demoted to space holders.

The library has turned from a space that treats books like treasures, where thick layers of dust protected knowledge, to a profane location where much happens and little is read. Revolutions don't always devour their children immediately. Sometimes they just suck them dry. Like a vampire that prefers to consume its victim slowly, rather than a monster that gobbles them down in one bite. The digital forces weaken their victims slowly until—still halfway intact on the outside, but completely devoid of energy on the inside—they collapse. Porn theaters, travel agencies and postcards have already lost their lives this way, and now libraries are in danger. With every Wikipedia page, every Google Book Scan they lose a grain of their aura, an ounce of their necessity. Jobs and funds are being cut.

Even though now would be the time for the library to position itself confidently against the intangible. Its allure comes from the endless rows, the battalions of spines. In the smallest space it offers visitors a cosmos of perspectives: Within it the reactionary has space next to the progressive, the exceptional stands back to back with the conventional. The library is a home to polyphony. In the glow of the green lamp shade you travel more safely than on any slick surfboard. The library as the departures hall. The books as the planes with their gangways extended. Patiently awaiting their sole passenger. At some point he will come, on a dark winter night and pull at random while strolling along the shelves. Then the engine starts and the plane lifts off.

"The library will close in fifteen minutes," the voice of an unemployed actress informs me. Via the intercom she wishes me a safe journey home. And at the exit they will probably offer hot towels and coconut water.

Where does it come from, this dull, snivelly feeling of having been born too late? To live in times without arias and excess? Time in which you want to plead with your parents: "Keep your memories to yourselves! Don't you realize how they crush our shoulders and our courage with their weight?"

Whenever I imagine the past, I picture how days started (maybe not quite with a gunshot wound, but at least with a bloody wet shave), the delicious anticipatory rage with which one opened the newspaper, downed the coffee and threw the one-night-stand off the sofa—how one loved loving with all its difficulty. Whenever I think of the past, I get envious. Because so much was destroyed that could be built anew. Nobody wants war, but we should have the freedom to dream of a fresh beginning. A time when adversaries existed, real enemies. When you weren't permitted to take the coward's route, to avoid saying hello. "You also have to greet those you don't know" (Karl Kraus). A time when we actually said things to each other's faces that left their marks. When real things were the subjects of discussions, not just states of affairs, when the arguments were about right and wrong, and the critical impulse manifested itself, thereby putting itself at stake.

We can no longer even imagine that people once believed—were fundamentally convinced— that things should and could be done in a radically different way.

Planning the great coup, together at the kitchen, bar, or cafeteria table, what kind of confidence and sense of mission would it have taken? What sense of power?—You are done, now it's our turn: We are coming to your schools, your parliaments, your factories, theaters, publishers, newsrooms and factory floors.

The revolt of our ancestors was not just spawned by a feeling. It strode on the high heels of theory, possessed intelligence, mental agility, had read much and with great concentration. It was able to criticize the current situation with turns of phrase that today we have to look up.

What and how intensely they dreamed, that is what I envy. I, who often sit across from them on the tram, silent, depressed by their advantage of experience. I, who am their inferior in terms of knowledge (how many books have I really read twice? and where are my notes on them?) and passion (slept with fewer women, never have been to Cuba, diligently kept the twenty mph speed limit). I, who stand by and listen to the stories of how great it was then. I envy their wounds. Their gazes, their longing. And their hairstyles. Why are there no more groups today who fly to Princeton? Why are there no more collectives, communes and tearooms? Is it really enough to lie around on Sunday afternoon with Alexandra and mark the vacation days in our shared calendar in blue? It is still our parents who wear the leather jackets.

Of course, everyone is always a successor. That's nothing new, the feeling that you've arrived too late. But the question is whether one is able to make something of this feeling--or whether one simply watches the candle burn down. This has never been about the majority, which has always toiled so that the few could govern, paint and write. The many have forever given the few a light without catching fire themselves. It has always been an elite, a small esoteric group that has been responsible for progress. Those who think too much about equality at the outset lose the courage to act. They will soon only make sure that the towel rests on the warm (but not too warm!) radiator and that the bike chain is well-oiled.

Now the security guards enter the reading room from the back. They start to clean off the tables of those who haven't been at their desks in the last thirty minutes. Carelessly the women shove everything left behind into yellow mailboxes—notes, books, photocopies. Once the desk is empty they spray it down with disinfectant from a silver can and polish it with a cloth until it's shiny.

We work and relax, driven by the attendance clock. That is our situation. We have never really lived, only felt the pull in our chest when we hear how old someone was when they put their stamp on history, when they created this or that. Somehow everyone seems to only have been in their mid-twenties when they wrote their first novel, played their first leading role, made their first million.

For me, envy means first and foremost: counting the years. Calculating how much distance there is, how much runway remains. It means: wanting to be Rimbaud. Wanting to live without the longing for the past. To be a creator, theater director, starter of a discourse if necessary, but to be there, really be there and not just sort through business cards in an office. As an eternal spectator, the shadow boxer who never entered the ring, always just dreaming of the music that would accompany the crowd cheering him on.

The last warning, a security guard approaches me with heavy steps and pulls away my chair. "Get out." The library as transitory space from which you are mercilessly evicted when the grace period is over. The cleaning crew approaches with their silver spray cans. This time the women are wearing masks over their mouths and have a vacuum cleaner, no, a pressure washer, in tow. Now it's the books' turn. Every day they are scrupulously cleaned until the last fleck of dust is obliterated. They shine like never before, these books, but they are no longer being read. The knowledge disappears along with the dust. The aura of touchability.

We lack the fire. The courage. We always come in second. We, who at night secretly write our own names into the books of our fathers, in the hope that the heritage will give us strength.

VI
LUXURIA

Two men in suits stroll past the entrance of a prewar building, their arms crossed behind their backs, like Greek philosophers. One keeps his shoulders straight, the other walks a little bent. They are wearing black masks and their foreheads are sweaty. They approach me, quietly. The neighbors aren't on good terms, they say, and guide me past a dark staircase and across a backyard without cats to an old wooden door with a milk glass window. "Knock three times, please. Have fun." A young woman opens the door, her gaze calculating, even as her mouth is smiling.

Her pale skin reflects the flickering candle light and I think I see her shivering. But later, at the end, when she will lie next to me on the table and stroke the back of my head, the shivering will be over. Then there will be only calm and happiness.

A dark garden of sequin and velvet, ghost lights, an oasis of ecstasy and music. Effervescent drinks and fresh exotic fruit. A ruby red basement where you can gamble—for luck, for money or for the head of Laocoön. A midsummer night among strange friends and friendly strangers. A little "Eyes Wide Shut." Just a little. The dream of a night in which everything is forgiven. In which you can lose the shame, can finally escape the old limpet that latched on in childhood days. Touching naked skin, shattering glasses, roaming labyrinths. Darkness and candles, a shadow from somewhere that becomes a friend, a lover for a brief time. And then moves on as if nothing had happened, as if this was all just a game and the bill would never come due. Though lips are sealed / Violins whisper / Care for me! I've had this dream for a long time. It snuck into my fantasy and followed me, expectantly and a little derisively, as if to say: you don't dare! In the deciding moment you will close your eyes, will adjust your bow-tie and remember that you will have to get up early on

Monday morning. You will look forward to a tax refund and the next physiotherapy appointment. And let the others give it a go.

I have always been better at dreaming of the big win than at actually placing the bet. More ambitious in drawing up maps and deciding on a direction, rather than putting the plan into action. The dream is my evasive maneuver, a never-fulfilling prophecy.

But tonight I want to change course, want to be rakish and odd. Let us dance, exchange looks and sit in the back room in the dark and kiss each other's necks. Let's do everything we want without fearing that anything will escape these walls.

Why always think of retreat when the lights go down? Would Fitzgerald have researched bus times as others were dancing the waltz? Come over, look into the mirror and stand up straight. Tomorrow you can return to being a harmless nobody.

Of all the things that are bad form, that counteract the senses and the longing, taking off the mask too early is the worst. A few ignoramuses do it only a few steps into the room, just to wipe their forehead or to scratch the corner of their eye. They fear the veil, the hidden glance.

But I, intent on living it all, intent on waking the sleeping song, hold tight to the desire for secrecy and keep the mask on. This is my night. Nothing will stop me. Not the mediocre EDM DJ, not the gay car salesman out on the hunt, not even the tired TV star who thinks he can pay for his drinks with his famous face.

A palm tree stands in the front corner, illuminated red, reminding me of the house in the south, the *casa* in a Spanish alley, where in the morning donkey carts clanged against the sidewalk and in the evening we drank wine on the rooftop terrace until the stars fell. In the interior courtyard there was a palm tree, the roots of which had crawled under the house, into the sewer and the well, had lifted the tiles and cracked the facade. One afternoon a *Palmista* arrived with three power saws and a sickle. He cut up the noble tree giant into ever smaller pieces until all that was left was a stump. We used it as a table, toasting civilization with a glass of Rioja. The house was forgotten, sold long ago, but the palm tree stuck with me, with its wild growth and great joy in its murderous embrace.

The tree here in the hall is its little sister. Standing shyly in the corner, allowing itself to be touched by the guests. But not moving its branches, indifferent to their embraces.

On the stage, the revue starts. A Burlesque dancer steps in front of a semicircle of costumed illuminati. In real life she's a clerk at a suburban bank, but tonight she's pulling the frills off her body. It's all well rehearsed. On the last note she drops her last piece of clothing. But contempt is written in her face, her tantalizing gaze is directed at the ceiling. A Salomé would look different. Where is the cut-off head, where the bloodthirst, the terrors of lust? Her skin, which I touch in passing with the tip of my finger, is cold. The revenge of the touched: to suffocate the embers with a shiver. Communicate to each admirer that someone else would do just as well.

Above the entrance to the basement, where the beer crates would normally be stacked high, a bare-chested young girl is now sitting on the windowsill, taking photographs. She does not respond to calls, doesn't let anyone get close. A malicious oracle, a false Loreley? In any case she remains there the entire night, even later when the bass has stopped and the police have confiscated all of the magic powder.

A broad-shouldered boy in suspenders makes an announcement, speaks with an Italian, Russian and Greek accent. Invites the crowd to a celebration with the ghosts of yesteryear and the demons of today. His girlfriend is from Madrid. She has tragic dark eyes and an Eton crop. When she speaks, she speaks in long sentences. Together we descend into the basement, while her boyfriend is busy with drinks and coke upstairs. Later I see him come down the stairs to watch me desire her. Where does it come from, this clandestine, malevolent and yet infinitely arousing male fantasy to see one's own lover in the arms of a stranger? To closely watch her surrender, how she puts her arms around his neck, her legs around his hips, her breath on his ear.

Upstairs the Russian DJ plays EDM sets that lack a sense of time and place. His music is too challenging. The people want Abba, not James Blake. A young woman of nobility, beautiful eyes, challenges a man in a fox mask to a round of arm wrestling. Last year, he slept with her, then shut the door on her. She would rather punch him in the face, no warning, break his nose. But it is too early for that. In a few hours she will get her revenge: She will make sure that he hears her moan as she makes love to a bearded musician on the bar. She will—just as his pants open in lust—notice with a satisfied glance that the man in the fox mask has been defeated, that the toxin of jealousy has done its work. Humiliated he will tumble out onto the street, to look up into the sky for a moment.

Outside, a grieving widow has placed a sign in front of the closed metal shutters. The name of her deceased husband is written on it in shy letters. She knows that he would have liked to stand at the bar, in the midst of the bustling crowd, in the twitching light. He would have been perfectly quiet, simply observing. His eyebrows slightly raised, lips pursed. He would have thought of Buñuel and Visconti and how much time he still had. He was the film critic for a major newspaper. Often he'd walk back and forth in the middle aisle of a cinema, unable to decide on a row. I once worked as a waiter at a birthday party in his house. I was fourteen and his daughter twelve. We bit each other's lips on the balcony and later I read in the newspaper of his death. There aren't a lot of people whose view on the world you miss. He was one of them.

Back in the basement, where an old sign says "suffocation hazard," red velvet is draped over waiters' lockers. The hum of the refrigerators fills the room. In front of them people play roulette at a long table. Nobody verifies date of birth; no account balance is checked. In the back corner, a young Austrian writer reads the intercessions that he has written for his godson. He is invited to his baptism tomorrow. He looks around in disgust, the players frozen with covetous desire as they lean across the table. The ball is rolling—*rien ne va plus*. The croupier, an Orientalist from Wales, is completely pale, but he's used to crazy nights. His favorite movie is *Just a Gigolo* with Marlene Dietrich and David Bowie. A princess and prince who never came together—the divide was too vast. They talked on the phone a few times, but Marlene didn't want to see David. He who wore the scent, the strong perfume of a new era. He wanted to come to her with a helicopter. A helicopter! She hadn't spent her life on the back of a piano to be picked up by half a man in a helicopter.

The girlfriend of the boy in suspenders wishes she had her very own Fallada, the little man and his burning question: "What now?" Wishes for a ballroom with ten thousand Chinese lanterns. Suspenders alone no longer do the trick. There would have to be neon advertisements and silk tablecloths. Signal lamps that can be activated with the push of a button that say either "Do Not Disturb" or "Dance Requests Welcome." What is missing here is not just the Champagne fountains and pickled herring pyramids. Most of all she is thinking of the table telephones that Fallada mentions. You could call anyone in the room with them. Could threaten, seduce, goad. *And when you're not in the mood to talk, you can write a letter and send it through a pneumatic tube.* In 1979 the Resi was demolished. Today you can go shopping at a Lidl there instead.

The pretty one with the Eton crop is rhapsodizing about pneumatic tubes. Last month, she deleted her Tinder account. She wanted to win back serendipity. She wanted to want to be surprised again. She would show Suspenders what he was missing. "To make him jealous once, just once. To feel his fearful look from the other side of the room. To see doubt in his face. Just once."

His mouth is greedily glued to foreign lips. He's a man without a sense for the question: "What now?" To feel grand in front of her, irresistible and wild, he has to go groping other women. Had to lick others' necks and push his hands into random strangers' sweaty underwear. *"I am a Man! Who more than I? / If any, let him spring."* These first lines of Schiller's poem are always at the ready when he has to justify his desire.

In the early days, there'd been the great promise of departure. The dream of endless evenings in the south. Someone who would count her freckles and protect her from mosquitoes, who would sail with her into the sunrise and never talk of skinnier girls. They had jointly picked out the suspenders, in a workwear shop in the harbor district of Athens. Later, on the ferry to Icaria, their lovemaking had been so intense, they nearly fell overboard. Not much remains. A few fierce exchanges and a first gray hair in the ear. She had dreamed of black and white family photos and of a wedding night in a tree house. But now he's been making out for hours with a busty noblewoman. The morning yoga on the carpet in their prewar apartment (not his, his mother's), the joint sweating and wheezing, hadn't been great for their love life. Neither had the shared toothpaste.

The roulette table is the meeting point for those out of luck. What they are missing in love must be attainable in a game. They put everything on black, their color of hope. My arm reaches for a female hip. Evolutionary biology designed it well: a chimpanzee baby can easily rest on the hip bone of his mother, to free her hands to search for food.

And not even jealousy is reserved for humans: the rhinoceros hornbill, one of the biggest hornbilled birds of the southeast Asian rainforests, who lives off fruit and large insects, uses his large beak primarily to wall in his pregnant mate, preventing her from leaving the nest. The only remaining opening is a small crack for feeding, which separates the female completely from the outside world. Locked into her treehouse prison she leads a sad existence. It is only when the young birds are fully fledged and the female has regenerated her plumage that the nesting hole is opened again. If the male dies in the meantime, the female and the young birds starve to death...

Finally, my arm finds the hip of the Fallada fan. Finally, something to hold onto on this noncommittal evening. In the cinema I have heard it as often as I have forgotten it in real life: The one sentence that says it all. That is reassuring and at the same time dangerous, direct and yet discreet, and it tends to mention "your eyes" or "your radiating smile." In any case, it is mostly just a sentence, a main clause without branches, in between the first glance and the first kiss. Only those who take the narrow strip of the first encounter with momentum have a chance.

I ask her about lust. About the words, the smells, the colors she associates with it. About the images. With a smile she brushes my arm off her hip and starts talking. Of Spain, of a bull fight, of a lavender field under the stars. Lust to her is the spring in their steps down to the lake, when they both know that in a moment all clothes and inhibitions will fall. Lust is the jump into the dark water, the first touch underneath the surface, the quiet whisper, close to the ear, she says. Resistance to her would be futile.

She smiles rakishly. Is that an offer? An invitation to continue? "And what about you?" she asks. I tell her about Rodin, about the bronze statue in Paris, the naked girl gathering her hair. Arms crossed overhead, back straight, chest out. Her eyes are closed. She dreams of a tender, tight embrace, coming out of nowhere and leading to nothing. She longs for Kleist's "Oh!". Romanticizes innocently and knows nothing of Freud and his demystifications.

I put my arm around her and tilt my head back. I used to button my shirt low, hoping I looked like James Dean. How he would walk on the dusty desert path in *Giant*, drunk and disgusted with his own life, the future bust, the end in sight. And then his shirt is unbuttoned by the wind. That, too, is lust, I say: the sweaty, dirty chest of a beautiful man. Sweat as a real promise, not the fake product from the gym.

She turns away with a smile, disappears into the bathroom. I stay behind and reassure myself: this is the intimacy I'm longing for, my wish for free lust within immediate reach.

The bed is the last space in which there are no rules, no conditions. You can devote and abandon yourself until the church bells ring and the bread and soft cheese arrive at the front door. Jeanne Moreau, the cigarette afterward, those were victory signs from a world in which you could be sure that the sun was the only witness.

"What do you miss?" someone once asked Beckett. His answer was: "Beauty."

But going for a walk in Hyde Park on a sunny late summer day, a journalist with him exclaimed how beautiful the day was and what a joy it was to live that precise moment, and Beckett supposedly said: "No sir, I wouldn't go that far."

Between beauty and despair there is only one word: lust. It cannot be provoked. Decorating the bathtub with tea candles and dried lavender doesn't help. Being naked doesn't prompt it either. Beautiful breasts can be cold. Strong arms can feel hollow. Those who intentionally search for lust will not find it. They will have to make do with a bit of greed, a bit of instinct. It doesn't come to the shower in the drunken morning hours when four friendly strangers are rubbing against each other. It doesn't come to palm trees or DJ rigs. Let alone roulette tables.

But then at the end, when everyone has left, removed their masks, somebody rubs my back with a warm hand. The girl from the milk glass window at the reception has waited for me, a stranger's soul in a dark forest. Two who got away, now lying next to each other among the shattered wine glasses. The dreams had all crashed. But then she entered through the door, turned off the light and dispelled the shame. Those who are found by lust won't be helped by velvet or exotic fruit. They are led away defenselessly. And won't be released from it easily. No matter how often the phone rings upstairs, no matter how heavily the branches beat against the window.

**VII
IRA**

Anger has dirt under its fingernails. It scratches the varnish, scratches and tears until the skin opens, until nerves are raw and exposed. Sitting at the stone table, playing cards? That is an image for later days. Before then, at twenty-five or twenty-six or twenty-seven, you have to talk big. Otherwise, you'll always speak in a whisper and the cards will never be reshuffled.

My mirror self sits next to me in the car. Not a friend, not a stranger. A man in between. The handshake has gotten agreeable over time. He briefly looks me in the eye, then past me, into the distance. He's not quite there yet, or a step ahead, already on to the next job, the next deal. He holds the steering wheel like a young entrepreneur, with one hand, as the left one hangs nonchalantly out the window.

Cars are not a matter of perspective. They've always been dirty, much too big, and there's never a parking spot nearby. Little Tree air fresheners sway from the rearview mirror like nasty traitors. The backrest leans too far back. The seat is scalding and the seatbelt warning chimes every second. The tank is almost empty and there's spilled milk in the trunk again. The car offers a refuge only for old men who like to spread their legs. Those who feel bossed around, constricted and emasculated by the current conditions. Those conditions have changed, worsened. Even secretaries are no longer what they once were. Only behind the wheel does the world still belong to those who once conquered it.

Our pockets are full. We share cars and points of view that we never longed to have, hurry from one late-arrival to the next—always with an excuse, a little one-liner—we've always had the feeling of being on the right side and will never understand how important it is to do the wrong thing first. To go full sail in the wrong direction, against the current, against the wind.

That's our misfortune. That we never knew how to start the day without a bowl of muesli on the table. Without wanting to please anyone. Without any tobacco that we can roll to prove to the world how basic we live. Natural smoking now means to sit cross-legged and to lick creased papers. The days of Marlboro cowboys riding without saddles are long gone. Their lassos are gathering dust in the stable. These days, they use electronic voice boxes.

When we met for the first time, one afternoon during the week in a cafe, the tension was palpable. He spoke fast and much and we immediately started dreaming together. Or rather: pretended to dream. Of an honest, sparking life. Of time. Of time we would use together to work on a blueprint, a manifesto. Nothing ever came of it. Not even a few lines in double-size font. Instead, many evenings when other things were more important. We held salons, threw parties, invited friends, introduced each other, talked, emptied other people's glasses. At the end, when we were each tucked into our freshly washed bedding, we sent each other a short text. Reassured each other that the real task still lay ahead, that we'd start working on it soon. "The age needs us," he once wrote. "Who if not us?" And I answered him, like Schiller would answer Goethe: "The last companions on a journey always have the most to say to each other." The only thing that offended me was that he always signed with his last name.

In the meantime, the others presented their books. Read at book launches in the sunset on roof decks. Described their everyday lives, their pain, their suffering and fake companionship. They found their own writing so funny. Had to giggle at every word, every syllable. In the end, it doesn't matter. Everything is encased in the bulletproof glass of irony. At these readings, we shot each other quick looks, convinced that our words would matter more. But we never wrote on these nights. Just that message again, the promise: More later.

Now he is sitting in the car (rented—what else?). He's driving and the clock is ticking along. The finish line is always in sight, a detour to Rome, but a real breakout doesn't happen this time either. This conversation, too, will stay clear of decisive turns. We had wanted to search for something that would shake up our lives, something worth fighting for. But now he tells me about his best friend's wedding. He was the best man. He wrote a long speech for him, even practiced it a few times in front of a mirror. And then, on the night of the wedding, at the dinner when he wanted to deliver it, the couple was caught up with the kids, constantly going off into the adjacent room to play Playmobil and count paper streamers. After dessert he made a last effort, but then the lights went out and the guests danced under the moonlight, accompanied by Britney Spears. The speech, the manuscript, he ended up leaving at the coat check, with a post-it: All best and till soon.

Having children is not enough. You have to make up a life along with it. Otherwise the child remains a golden calf around which the parents are dancing as if mad. He says and sighs loudly.

I listen. I concur. We can always agree on a counter position. But we keep postponing our own blueprint. Maybe there is no longer a need for utopias. Maybe a life without longing for a future is possible. Maybe it's not just possible but expedient? Finally grab the lid and take the pot off the stove. It has been boiling long enough, the old ideological soup… As he is talking like this, forming sentences as if they could also mean something entirely different, as if they were just exchangeable and without a deeper meaning, I feel doubt creeping up again. My doubt of him. And of myself. Because over time he has become my mirror. I saw in him what counts. Or rather: what I thought counted.

Once on a summer evening on the balcony at the goodbye party for a mutual friend, a young man from Syria joined us. Electrical engineer with certificates. In Germany for a year and already he had a real joke up his sleeve: "The road to hell is paved with government forms." The institutions didn't want to recognize his qualifications, and so he—former CEO of his own company in Syria—had to start over as an apprentice. On the night of his escape he had to leave behind his parents and wife, his family shredded by bullets. No last look into their faces, no goodbye, no chance for revenge. Just away, off into strange lands. And there he was and couldn't help it, he had to tell us, awful stories but in a soft voice. He read a poem to us, first in Arabic, then in German. And we drank beer, stood alongside and didn't know what to do.

Searched for reassurance in each other's eyes. I admired and loved my friend for this, that in this moment he wasn't too quick to offer his condolences, didn't make random pitying statements toward him, whose tale made us swallow our jokes. All he did was pull his hands out of his pockets, as if to spring to attention in front of this man, who bears his fate proudly, as others do their medals.

These were always only isolated moments. The times in which I felt trust in him. Respect even. I liked his way of speaking, always a little too fast, always a little rough, as if to show that he didn't have to prove anything. He never showed off with his language. Never used words that were too big for him, or seemed borrowed. He rented cars, but the words he wanted to own. I liked him, because he boasted with things that had long lost their importance for others. With sports, for example. His successes as a boxer, his tough right-handers. He proudly told of often getting unbidden invites to competitions, like an editor who might brag about how many unsolicited manuscripts they receive every day.

And with his passion for women. Whenever I met him, he had just had a fight with his Russian girlfriend, who suspected him of cheating, threw his things out the window or simply left. It often happened that she called him and yelled at him loud enough for everyone to hear. Then sometimes I would take the phone from him and talk her down like a little child that had just woken up in the house alone.

I'm sure he cheated on her. But I always held a protective hand over him. Because I knew that he didn't mean to cheat on her, but that he just wanted to see himself as an adventurer. I took this Catholic shortcut with him. Others might have called it Machismo, but I thought of *Last Tango in Paris*. There was one thing we agreed on: The world as it was could use a little more magic. Enchantment was to be one of our keywords, should ideally appear in the first paragraph. Marinetti had written "a roaring car that seems to run on grapeshot is more beautiful than The Victory of Samothrace." Instead I had hoped we would be writing of the beauty of the glowing meadow. Of the necessity to step out of the gloomy data thicket, where you can no longer even find the starting point.

But eventually, my hope was lost. After a final dinner with him, in which there was a lot of big talk, as usual, my doubts grew about whether he was the right one to get the ball rolling.

And now we are sitting in the car and he's talking about how much he had to drink the night before, how high his blood alcohol might still be. And somehow our conversation lands on the big question. And suddenly he makes a dismissive remark about my attempts to put the dissatisfaction into words, says something like: "It's always just about the revolution—you repeat yourself and there are no consequences. You need to keep your nose to the grindstone, otherwise nothing will ever come of it." He says this with such clarity, with so much venom that I would love to tear off the windshield wipers and stuff them down his throat. My head is spinning and I ask him to stop the car.

Sometimes a wrong word, a wrong sentence is all it takes to forever lose trust. A night, half asleep at half past two, can set the course for your life. A careless confession, a wrong name at the wrong place at the wrong time, and suddenly the path that just seemed wide open is blocked forever. The wrath that attacks, that sneaks out from the core and digs into every perceptible fiber. And when the wrath is there, when it has been called, it's hard to get under control.

Wrath seems to be an emotion from a different time. It makes you think of comic strips or family fathers in the fifties. It has been a long time since anyone mentioned the wrath of God.

The New Testament was a better fit for our time, a Protestant minister recently said. As if you could just subsume the inscrutable into the state of shallow contentment, in which the flags forever fly at half-mast, without anyone being able to say what is being mourned.

Wrath has become a pathology. The angry person is a radical endangering the comfortable emotional state of the masses. Never was consensus valued as highly as it is today.

In the wide squares of Athens and Rome the anger of the young orator was the litmus test of his character. Those who weren't at least once shaken by anger, who didn't tear their clothes and stomp their heels sharply into the ground, were viewed with suspicion by Greeks and Romans. Seen as vain dazzlers, good-for-nothings. Today the opposite is true: Those who are angry are regarded as nuts. Those who speak of wrath are placed under suspicion, labeled anti-democrat. We doubt the status quo so little, are so addicted to harmony, that every impulsive thought seems dangerous to us. The ideal of opposition has deteriorated to a flimsy gesture.

When Stefan Zweig—1940 in Brazil at a writers convention—was pressed by the journalists to speak out, to draft a pamphlet against Hitler, he refused. He, the Jew, who had been displaced and humiliated, exiled and betrayed, replied: "Gentlemen, I cannot write against something, I can only write for something." Zweig spoke about the futility of resistance when surrounded by those who all think like you. In a situation in which everyone is of the same opinion from the start, the call for resistance is meaningless, since it doesn't bear any consequence. Only where you're in a minority, where the rallying cry of the others sound louder, only here is resistance a heroic deed.

Now the car is parked and we walk a little, side by side, under the tall beech trees. The path is scattered with puddles and the air is heavy from the rain. It's not even rain, just a dull dripping from the leaves. Drops, drops, nothing but drops.

Back in school, when someone insulted my mother, I would always punch them in the face. A little spitefulness was all it took to provoke me. Essentially I was just waiting for an opportunity to prove my courage, to display my fighter's morale to the gallery. That others saw how I defended my mother's honor has always been important to me. My heroic act needed spectators. Wounds were only useful if I could show them off to somebody.

But today, in the rainy reprieve I lack the drive, can't even hold my head up straight. And that despite the fact that there is no greater insult to me than "keep your nose to the grindstone." This offhand remark from the squinched mouth that questions—no, dismisses!—everything I believe in, everything I feel and think, everything I wrestle to put into words. In hindsight, every word that

I've addressed to him feels like being exposed against my will. The important thing had always been that we'd protect the other's pathos. Protect it against the sceptics, side by side. The was our deal: that we'd be allowed to lose ourselves together and seclude ourselves in our shared feeling. And now?

I want to scream at him, want to throw my disappointment at his feet, want to tear the backpack from his shoulder and kick him in the back of his knee: you who shares cars and views with the world, who is barely above it all, who in truth would like to have kids already, you just think of warm bathtubs and beach vacations. You, who pretend to be a boxer in your free time so you won't have to face the fight in your real life. Will you end up being one of those who are happy to settle for a well-trodden path? Didn't you want to invent your own language with new words and tones? Instead you spend your weekends in the swimming pools of former State Secretaries and print menus for your next birthday party. "All this talk of narratives puts me to sleep," you once said. And the "time of the hyperrationalists" was coming to an end. You cared about meaning, about impact, about power. Nothing of that has remained. Your force has run out like oil from a rusty canister. Stay your course, talk with your girlfriend as if she were a child and tell the whole world that you are working on something big. Allow yourself to be blindfolded and finish off other people's drinks. You can always be against something. And being for something you can always save for later. That's what I'd like to yell— but I remain silent and stand up straight.

And maybe he's right. Maybe dreaming no longer is enough at some point. When all wonder is used up, righteousness is all that's left. Then even feelings are refutable.

He sits on a graffitied park bench and crosses his legs. All strength is gone from his features. All magnetism faded. What remains is someone who I wouldn't even want to give my left hand. Someone I look past like a stranger at a bus stop. I was wrong about him; I fell for him like the golden-framed ad in a travel catalogue.

I turn my straight back to him and go on by myself. He used to be mine. Now he is no one.

The trip is now mine alone. I let my feet carry me. The city has emptied out. In the shops only the ads are blinking. At the end, time will be the winner. Because it keeps running. Even if we all succumb to sleep—it completes the course. Leaves the dreamers behind in their sorrow, the knowledge that each of us is made of two—as

Marivaux says, "One who reveals himself, and one who conceals himself."

The doubt sits on my shoulder from now on, has latched on. Makes sure that I don't revert to a carefree state, don't say again with great satisfaction: I am too young! Regardless, I don't want to apologize for my hopes. Not yet. Until I turn thirty I'm allowed to talk and plan, question and desire as much as I want. And write without fear of mistakes. Until I am thirty.

The seven nights of sins were seven nights against the time. They postponed my trial for a moment. I have seen what it means to mature. Have passed through many shapes and asked children's questions. I searched for meaning and expression, I drew shapes in the sand. Against the emptiness. So that something remains.

Maybe like Rilke put it: "Be ahead of all parting, as if it had already happened." You don't always have to look back to part with something. Sometimes looking ahead can be sadder than looking back. I'm still standing on the side of the road. In the last shadow. But the sun is climbing higher. Soon the first ray of light will hit me. I can already see the ghosts on the other side of the road, rolling the dice for my future. Playing with my heart. In a moment everything will be set. The winner will have been determined.

Then I will take my first step into the road. I will step out of the protective night and into the gleaming light of day. Surrender to my Curriculum Vitae. Satisfy the ghosts. You will see.

But until then let me draw in the sand one last time. Leave a trace for all those who can still be moved. I have written this for them. A text of fear. Fear of the transition. Mostly of hope, though. Hope that there are still things to come. I'll wait. Here on the side of the road in the last shadow. Soon I'll have to cross. Soon it'll be too late.

BEFORE THE END

Dear S,

Congratulations, you have passed the maturity test. Welcome, now you're one of us. In the meantime, winter has arrived. It will harden you for what is to come. If it is to come for you. Because that's the first lesson—there is little that still awaits: wedding, kids, a job, sure. But they are not waiting for you. From now on, you have to make everything happen yourself. And let me tell you, the worst thing is, you can't surprise yourself. The only surprise left is death.

I'm sorry, your stories made me emotional and moody. I'm sad that it's over. Angry, too. Because I had expected so much.

A young man takes a maturity test to avoid growing up. To protect his feelings from too much protection. I'd never heard of such a wish. And in all honesty, didn't think it was possible. That it is really possible to protect yourself from it.

Indeed, you have completed your assignments so dutifully that I think you are well prepared for a job, and to become a husband, father and role model. But I am not angry or sad for you. I am sure you will be glad to assume the position the world has ascribed to you. To belong. Maybe not squarely in the middle. A bit off to the side, probably to the left (or right?) as a sincere, critical spirit.

I am angry and sad because I had expected so much. For myself. Because I had hoped to get instructions for a counterweight to my life—wife and dog and routine. Sadly, in vain.

Because where in this text are the thoughts, the sentences, the formulas that can save me when necessary? What are the changes you have effected, where are the traces you have left, what impression did you make, against whom did you rebel, what new era did you start? Was the distinctiveness of your vision not just the color of the light, sometimes night blue, angry red at other moments. No heavy blow, no real threat, no new beginning. Nothing that compelled me to defect from everything I have believed up to now.

Maybe I'm doing you wrong. But I really did what I could. I have had you fed, had you rise and fall, I have made you comfortable, exposed you to your past and demanded your future. I aroused your greed, stimulated your senses and nerves, distracted and rerouted you. I remote controlled you and questioned you about your freedom. I wanted you tired so you wouldn't censor yourself. I didn't offer you any protection other than that of the night. I wanted to expose you to danger, most of all the danger of failure.

But you didn't fail, you didn't come away injured. And I really believed: My test is going to be harder than those you have completed before. More difficult, more unpredictable. I was mistaken. Not about you, but mostly about myself.

When I read your night's story in the morning after walking the dog, I suddenly lacked all energy, was unwilling to complete the day's duties. But I was also at a loss because I no longer knew what to do or avoid if I were to follow you. I was always quick to agree to escapades in our shared sinful time. They cost me my wife. And now I only see the dog on weekends. But, and this is the worst thing: nothing has changed.

Don't mind me when I tell you to not trust that feeling, which you believe to be the gateway back into wonderland. It is unsteady and easily frightened, a spoiled brat. If you follow it, it will lead you around by the nose, block your way in the decisive moment. And if you need it, it will abandon you.

I'm not worried about you. Your Curriculum Vitae that you fear so much has long been drafted and this constitutes a new entry.

So you will move to a different city. You will need a new apartment. If you want, I can help. A friend of mine is moving out. Freshly renovated, centrally located, spacious, sunny and it has a balcony. The walls are white. You will like it.

If you had really hoped to acquit yourself through these seven nights from all that is coming, from your own expectations of yourself, then let me tell you: you were wrong. The clock will not stop at SEVEN. "More later," this excuse will continue to haunt you. The responsibility that you will bear will not make your free, least of all from your desire to return to the grass-green bygone days, which will get younger and younger the more you age.

Every time you look back at it, that late-summer day when we met for the first time will shine more brightly. To me it already seems like a distant time: How we sat there and ate. In the heat. Sweat on our foreheads, dripping down the backs of our knees. We cooled our throats with Burrata and Bresaola, Aperol Spritz and beer. But most of all, we talked. And you, with your open shirt and upturned collar, started talking about the stairs you are seeking. The stairs to the secret society for all those who still believe in secrets.

First I smiled, because it's refreshing to feed off the high spirits of someone so naive. Especially with the heat making it difficult to form a coherent thought. I could have watched you forever, as you effortlessly plucked the words from the air and stacked them on your plate until the rim was no longer visible.

At the end, I promised on a whim to hold your stirrups and swing the whip for you. I would be able to fulfill your desire for secrets and an alternate world. But you would have to deliver something in return: Seven nights. Seven sins. Seven utopias. We pushed back our chairs and that sealed the deal. I paid the bill.

Then, we were strangers. Now we know each other no longer by name only. We have spelled each other out, uncovered a few secrets. What we admire in each other is not magic. Our gaze is more trained. You will no longer surprise me.

I'll soon come and visit you in your new life. And for an evening, we can pretend to be dreaming again. Of one last summer. Freedom, no shackles, no worries.

But in truth, there is no way back for us to that late-summer day, even if the map is buried somewhere deep in your writing. Hopefully others will attempt the undertaking we have planned. It is definitely worth a try. This world could certainly use more of those who inhabit the clouds, more real dreamers.

The good thing is that now that you are on this side of the street, we will see more of each other. And we will empty a few more glasses— no doubt about that.

As wise men once liked to say:
Good night and good luck!

Your T